T0131884

Austrian Went Yodeling

GRACE MADRID

ILLUSTRATIONS BY:
VINCENT MADRID

To order additional copies of this book, contact:
Xlibris
1-888-795-4274
www.Xlibris.com
Orders@Xlibris.com

Illustrations by: Vincent Madrid

ISBN: Softcover   978-1-7960-6928-0
        Hardcover   978-1-7960-6929-7
        EBook   978-1-7960-6927-3

Print information available on the last page

Rev. date: 11/06/2019

Austrian Went Yodeling

GRACE MADRID

ILLUSTRATIONS BY:
VINCENT MADRID

This Fingerplay was always a favorite in my preschool classes. Children wanted to sing over and over again. We always had so much fun with the chorus, yodeling away:

With an avalanche… rumble, rumble

With the skier… swish, swoosh

With a grizzly bear… "Grr," growl

With three girl scouts… "Anybody want to buy Girl Scout cookies?"

With a preacher man… "Amen!"

Oh-Dee-A!... Oh-Dee-A-Hee Hee

I-Oh-Dee-A-Who Who

Oh Dee-A Hee Hee I-A

Twas an Austrian... went yodeling
on a mountain so high

Twas an Austrian … went yodeling on a mountain so high.

When he met with an avalanche interrupting his cry.

Chorus: (Roll hands together
for avalanche)

Oh-Dee-A! … Oh-Dee-A-Hee Hee

I-Oh-Dee-A-Who Who

Rumble, rumble

Oh Dee-A Hee Hee I-A

Twas an Austrian… went yodeling on a mountain so high.

When he met with a skier interrupting his cry.

Chorus: (swipe hand in front of you)

Oh-Dee-A!...Oh-Dee-A-Hee Hee

I-Oh-Dee-A-Who Who

Rumbel, rumble

Swish…swoosh

Oh Dee –A Hee Hee I-A

Twas an Austrian… went yodeling on a mountain so high.

When he met with a grizzly bear interrupting his cry.

Chorus: (hands curled into claws)

Oh-Dee-A!...Oh-Dee-A-Hee Hee

I-Oh-Dee-A-Who Who

Rumbel, rumble

Swish…swoosh

"Grr" growl

Oh Dee-A Hee Hee I-A

Twas an Austrian went yodeling on a mountain so high.

When he met with three girl scouts interrupting his cry.

Chorus: (hands on hips shouting, "Anybody want to buy girl scout cookies?")

Oh-Dee-A!...Oh-Dee-A-Hee Hee

I-Oh-Dee-A-Who Who

Rumbel, rumble

Swish…swoosh

"Grr" growl

"Anybody want to buy Girl Scout cookies?"

Oh Dee-A Hee Hee I-A

Twas an Austrian went yodeling on a mountain so high.

When he met with a preacher man interrupting his cry.

Chorus: (hands up in the air then bring them down)

Oh-Dee-A!...Oh-Dee-A-Hee Hee

I-Oh-Dee-A-Who Who

Rumbel, rumble

Swish…swoosh

"Grr" growl

"Anybody want to buy Girl Scout cookies?"

"Amen!"

THE END

About the Author

My name is Grace Madrid and I have worked in a preschool setting for more than twenty-four years. I have an AAS degree in Early Childhood Education and a Child Development Associate. I retired last year and have decided to write children's books. When I was teaching, I felt there was not a lot of resource books for the young child on some subjects for example; social and emotional, bullying, character counts, stranger danger and etc. My work as a teacher was very challenging and rewarding to me. I have enjoyed working with young children and being a part of their learning process, helping them learn about themselves and the world around them.

Meet the Illustrator

My loving grandson Vincent Madrid is responsible for bringing this fingerplay to life with his detailed illustrations which were created with water colors. Vincent started this project with me at the age of 12. For his young age he is an accomplished artist. His pieces have been selected for many art shows since he was in 3rd grade including annual art festivals, school district office displays and in 2018 he was chosen by the Catholic Diocese of Phoenix for his representation of "The Blessed Mary and Jesus" to meet Bishop Thomas Olmstead and discuss his drawing. Vincent spends many hours expressing his art work through various methods including sketching, painting and water colors. Vincent looks forward to continue working with his Grandmother, Grace Madrid, to produce more timeless childhood stories for young children just as he enjoyed at their age.

NOTES

This book belongs to

Printed in the United States
By Bookmasters